W9-CLR-467

MY CROCODILE DOES NOT BITE

For Franny —J.K.

Carolrhoda Books
A division of Lerner Publishing Group, Inc.
241 First Avenue North
Minneapolis, MN 55401 U.S.A.

Website address: www.lernerbooks.com

Main body text set in HandySans Regular 20/20.5.
Typeface provided by MADType.

Library of Congress Cataloging-in-Publication Data

Kulka, Joe.
     My crocodile does not bite / written and illustrated by Joe Kulka.
        p.   cm.
     Summary: Ernest enters his talented crocodile in the school pet show.
  ISBN: 978-0-7613-8937-8 (lib. bdg. : alk. paper)
     [1. Crocodiles as pets—Fiction. 2. Pets—Training—Fiction. 3. Humorous
  stories.] I. Title. III. Title: Dinobaseball.
  PZ7.K9490153My 2012
  [E]—dc23   2012017627

Manufactured in the United States of America
1 - DP - 12/31/12

8/13

MY CROCODILE DOES NOT BITE

Joe Kulka

CAROLRHODA BOOKS

MINNEAPOLIS

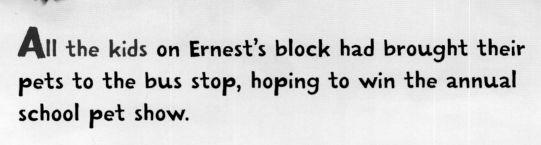

All the kids on Ernest's block had brought their pets to the bus stop, hoping to win the annual school pet show.

"I don't know why you all even bothered to bring those mangy animals. My dog Fifi is obviously going to win the ribbon," declared Cindy Lou.

Her little poodle growled in agreement.

Ernest showed up that morning with a **gigantic crocodile** tied to a rope.

"That's the ugliest dog I ever saw!" said Cindy Lou.

"He's not a dog. He's a crocodile. His name is Gustave," said Ernest.

"What a stupid pet," said Cindy Lou. "You can't bring him to school. He'll bite everybody!"

"Today's the school pet show." said Ernest. "If you can bring your dog, I can bring my crocodile. Besides . . ."

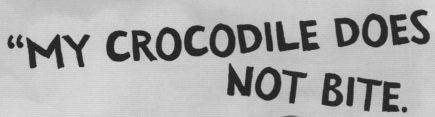

"MY CROCODILE DOES NOT BITE.

He's very well trained.
Can your dog do this?"

Ernest snapped
his fingers.

"Of course my dog can sit. She just . . . doesn't want to," said Cindy Lou.

The bus pulled up.

"Mr. Bus Driver!" Cindy Lou cried. "You can't let that crocodile on the bus. It will bite everybody!"

"MY CROCODILE DOES NOT BITE!

He's very well trained!" said Ernest. "He'll just sit quietly on the floor, like this." Then Ernest clapped his hands.

"Sorry, Ernest," said the bus driver. "I'm afraid
I can't let you bring your reptile onto the bus.
He just won't fit."

Ernest smiled back.
"Not a problem."

Ernest climbed onto the neck of his crocodile.
He waved as he rode off, yelling, "I bet we
even get there first!"

Gustave skittered across lawns
and through vegetable patches.
Ernest and his crocodile easily
beat the bus to school.

Cindy Lou came running off the bus to find a group of children petting Gustave.

"Stay away! That monster bites!" she warned.

"MY CROCODILE DOES NOT BITE!

He's very well trained. Look what he can do." Ernest whistled. The crocodile ran over and gave him a hug.

"Big deal. My dog comes when I call her too. She just . . . doesn't want to right now," said Cindy Lou.

"Okay. But can your dog do this?" Ernest pulled three tennis balls from his pocket. Gustave started wagging his tail.

"Big deal. Your crocodile eats tennis balls," sighed Cindy Lou.

"**Keep watching,**" said Ernest.

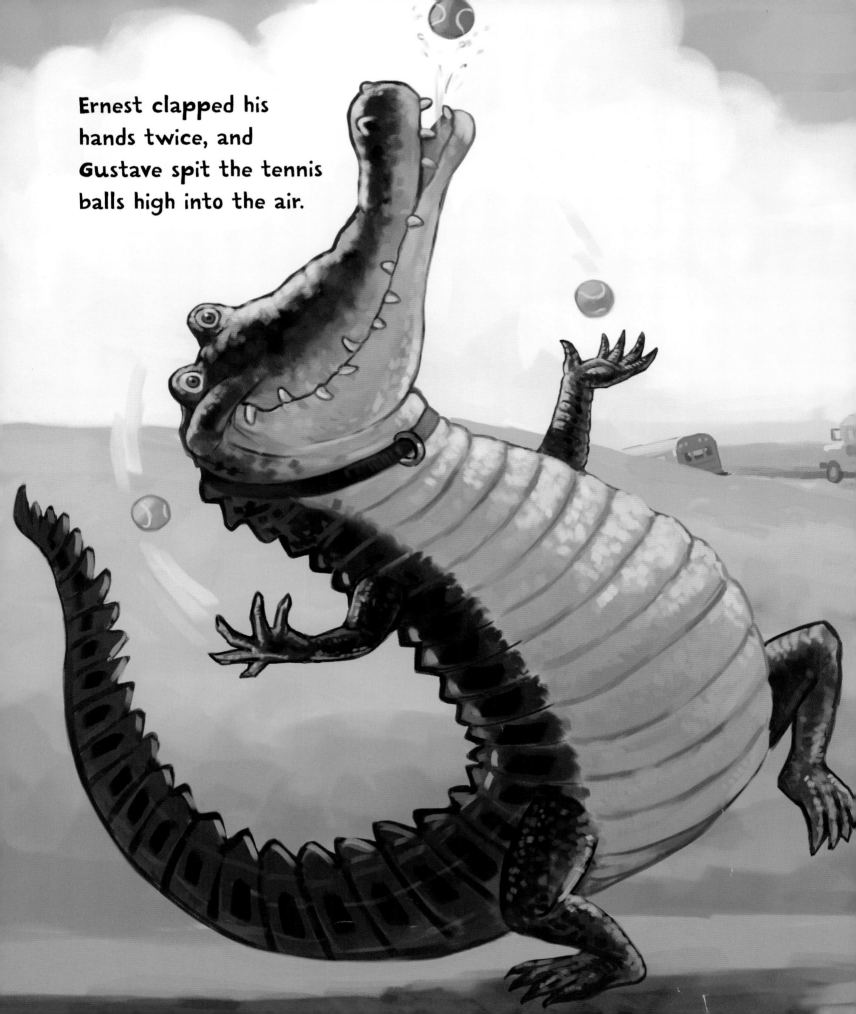

Ernest clapped his hands twice, and Gustave spit the tennis balls high into the air.

"There's more!" exclaimed Ernest. He reached farther into his backpack and pulled out a unicycle.

Everyone cheered. The principal, Mrs. Browne, laughed and danced.

"I forgot his hat and harmonica!" said Ernest.

Cindy Lou just glowered.

As the crocodile pedaled by **Cindy Lou**, she swiftly kicked the unicycle. Gustave came crashing down, tennis balls flying everywhere.

"Cindy Lou! That was a nasty, mean, dirty trick!" said Mrs. Browne.

"It was an accident! I was afraid the crocodile was going to bite me!" Cindy Lou replied.

Ernest looked worried. "I think Gustave swallowed his harmonica. And my crocodile does NOT bite! He's very well trained. Watch this."

Ernest tapped on Gustave's snout, and the crocodile opened his huge jaws.

Everyone cheered. Except, of course, Cindy Lou.

"Wow, Ernest!" said the principal.
"That really IS a well-trained crocodile!"

Cindy Lou couldn't take it anymore. "Look, everybody! My pet does tricks too. Fetch, Fifi!"

And this time, Fifi listened.

But Cindy Lou's tennis ball bounced off the school wall and rolled right into Gustave's open mouth.

Cindy Lou ran over and kicked the crocodile.
"Stupid reptile. Give me back my dog!"

She got down on her hands and
knees and crawled inside the
crocodile's mouth.

"Fifi! Get out of there!"

Suddenly, Gustave lifted his head into the air. With one big gulp, he swallowed up Cindy Lou.

"See?" said Ernest.

"MY CROCODILE DOES NOT BITE..."

"He swallows his food whole."

There was some disagreement later whether Ernest had clapped twice before the crocodile gulped down Cindy Lou.

There was no disagreement, however, that **Gustave** was indeed one well-trained crocodile.

DATE DUE